To the moon

'YIPPEE!'

written by **Jay Dale**

illustrated by Michelle Dybing

Gran and Carlos went
in a big red bus.

"Where are we going, Gran?" said Carlos.

"We are going to the park,"
she said.

Gran and Carlos went
in a big red train.

"Where are we going, Gran?"
said Carlos.

"We are going to the shops," she said.

Fruit & Vegetables

Gino's PIZZA

Gran and Carlos went
in a big red car.

"Where are we going, Gran?"
said Carlos.

"We are going to the beach," she said.

Gran and Carlos went
in a big red rocket.

"Where are we going, Gran?"
said Carlos.

"We are going to the moon!
Come on!" she said.